ELAINE'S STEM ADVENTURE

Hello, I'm Elaine and I'm going to be a scientist when I grow up. I decided that I'll be a scientist one day in school. My favorite teacher Mrs. Ferguson let us do so many activities in her class. She teaches Science and it is my favorite class. We use a lot of equipment, technology, engineering and a lot of math.

We learn to do things in order from beginning to end. We get our results and if it's wrong we try again.

We use the scientific method and its so much fun. Following each step will get the experiment done.

Step 1. Ask a question

Step 2. Do background research

Step 3. Construct a hypothesis

Step 4. Test your hypothesis by doing an experiment

Step 5. Analyze the data and draw a conclusion

Step 6. Share your results

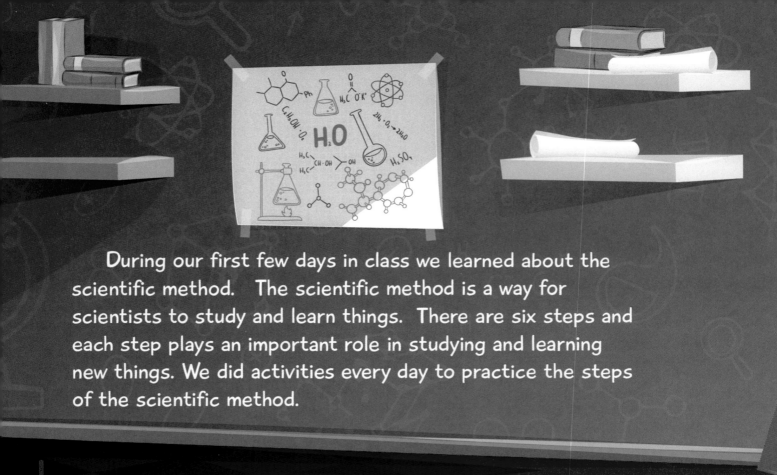

During our first few days in class we learned about the scientific method. The scientific method is a way for scientists to study and learn things. There are six steps and each step plays an important role in studying and learning new things. We did activities every day to practice the steps of the scientific method.

OBSERVE:

WHICH
WHY
WHERE

T ?
N ?

H₂SO₄

H₂O

On day one we were told the first step is to observe. We learned that when we observe, we take a closer look at something and ask questions. Mrs. Ferguson said that our questions should start with words like How, What, When, Who, Which, Why, or Where? For example, which object is heavier? Which of these four balls will role the furthest?

Mrs. Ferguson put us in groups of three and we began to observe items in the class room. My partners Samantha, Miles and I looked all around the room. We all saw a mysterious object in a jar and wondered what it was. Our question was: What is this item? Is it a liquid, solid or gas?

On the next day I was so excited to go to class. We would learn about the second step. The second step is to do research on the topic. Mrs. Ferguson said we have to do some critical thinking. She had us talking together about what we already know about the questions we are asking. She also took us to the library to find books about our topic. We also went to the computer lab and looked at videos about our topic.

Desk

Ball

SOLIDS

Wood

Toy

We found books on the states of matter. I learned that matter is everything that has weight and takes up space. Matter includes solids, liquids and gases and all of these items can be found in any place. Solids are made of a lot of little particles called molecules. In a solid object the molecules are packed very closely together. Solids have three main properties. A solid has definite volume, definite weight and definite shape that do not easily change.

Lake

Glass of w

Puddle

LIQUIDS

Pipette fluid

Drop

Samantha focused on the liquid. She told us that liquids have three main properties. A liquid does not have a definite shape, a liquid has a definite mass and a liquid has a definite volume. We learned that a liquid will always take up the same amount of space and take the shape of its container. An example is that water takes the shape of the cup you put it in.

Water flow

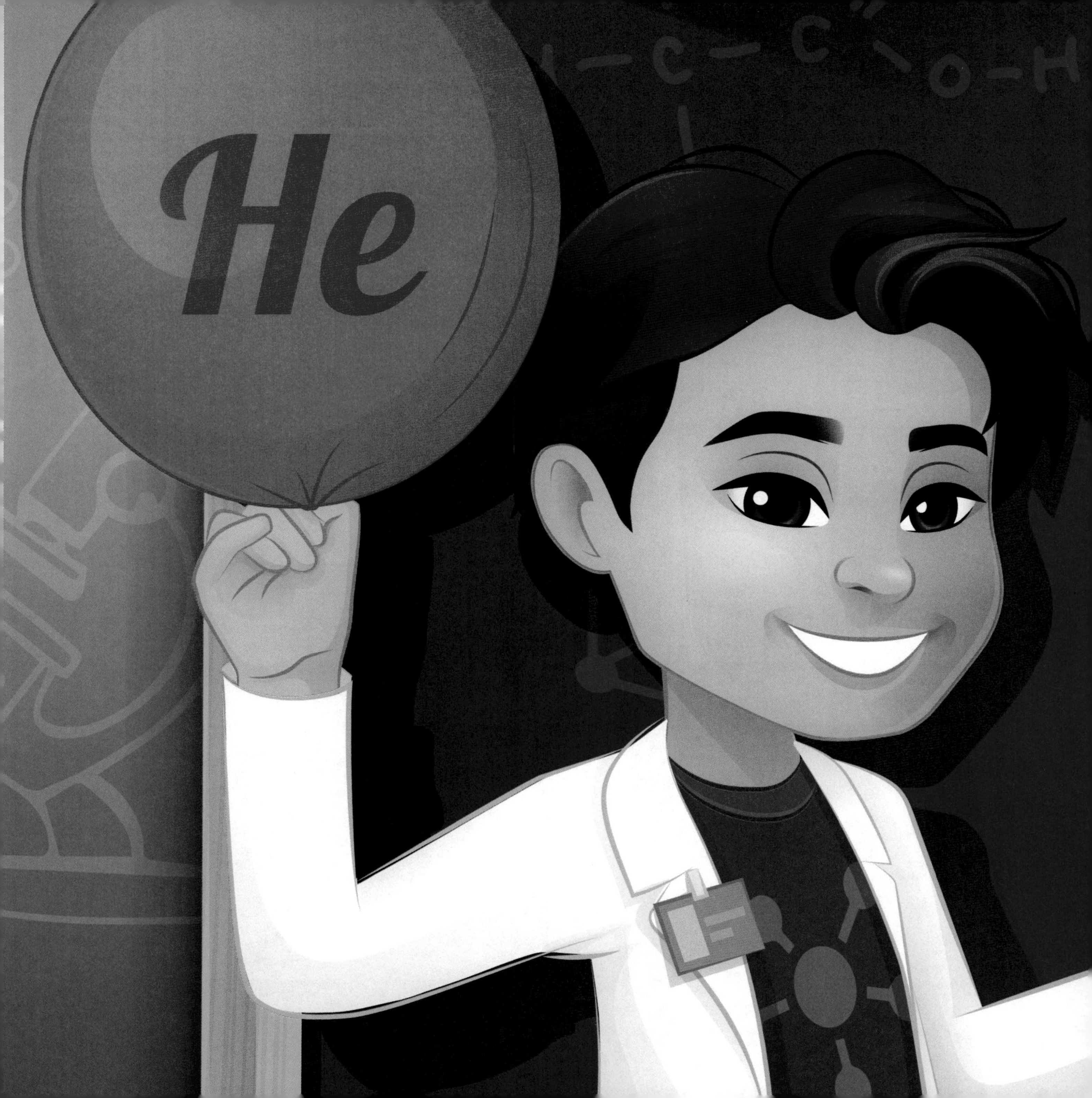
He

GAS

Wind

Balloons

Empty jar

Miles did research on gas. A gas has these three main properties. A gas does not have a definite shape, a gas does not have a definite mass and a gas does not have a definite volume. A gas does not always weigh the same or take up the same amount of space. However, like a liquid, a gas will always take the shape of its container, no matter the size or shape of that container. An example of this is helium in a balloon.

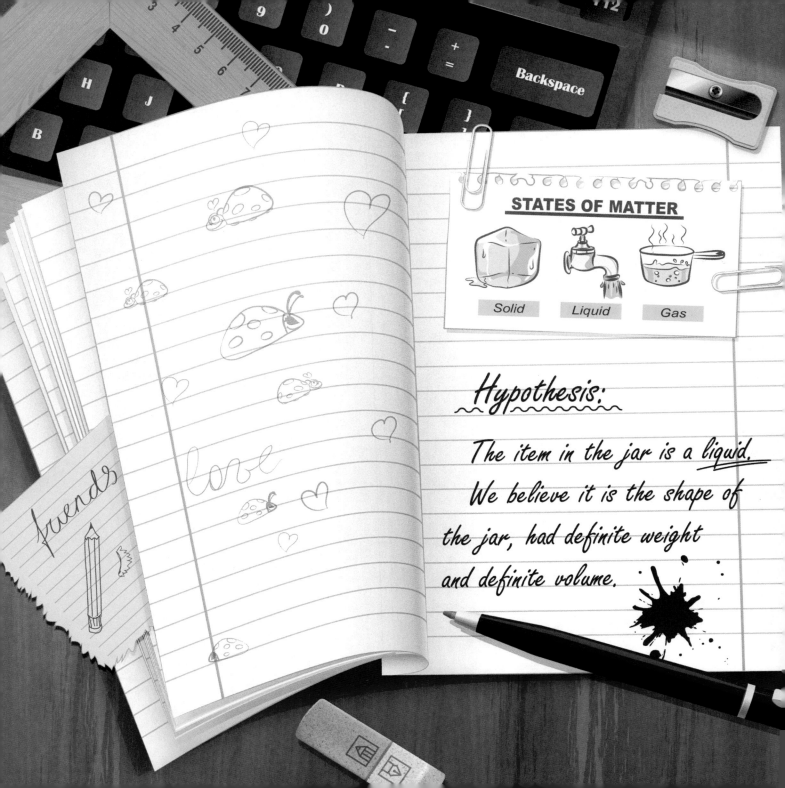

STATES OF MATTER

| Solid | Liquid | Gas |

Hypothesis:

The item in the jar is a liquid. We believe it is the shape of the jar, had definite weight and definite volume.

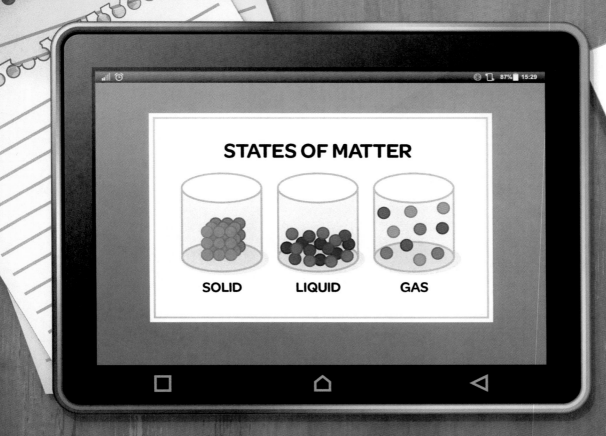

STATES OF MATTER

SOLID   LIQUID   GAS

We went to the library and to the computer lab. It took us two days finish all of our research. On day two we did most of our research. On day three we completed our research and completed step three, constructing a hypothesis.

Mrs. Ferguson said a hypothesis is nothing more than a good guess at an answer to the question from step one. Miles, Samantha and I decided our hypothesis would be: The item in the jar is a liquid.

We believe it is the shape of the jar, had definite weight and definite volume.

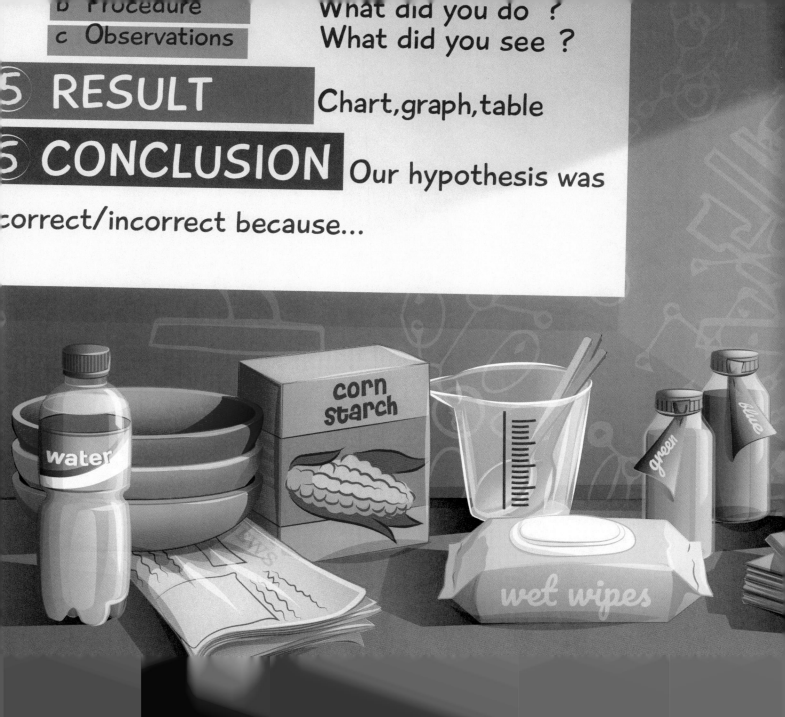

On the fourth day, we began step four. Step four is testing your hypothesis by doing an experiment. In order to do our experiment we had to gather materials, follow a procedure which we learned is a way to do things step by step, take detailed notes and try your experiment 3 times which scientist call trials, to test your hypothesis.

During our research we asked Mrs. Ferguson what materials where used to make the mystery jar. So when it came time to get our materials we were prepared. We got old newspaper, three bowls, three big spoons, a measuring cup, wet wipes, napkins, food coloring with red, green and blue, a box corn starch and two bottles of water.

During trial 1, we lined the table with newspaper so we wouldn't make a mess. Miles put 2 cups of corn starch in a bowl. Then I added 1 cup of water in the bowl. I then added a few drops of red color. Samantha stirred up our ingredients. At first the mixture was a little lumpy and Samantha kept stirring. After a few more stirs our mystery substance was finally ready.

Miles was the first person to touch it. His hand went straight to the bottom of the bowl and his hand was covered in stuff. When he pulled his hand out, the substance was dripping. Samantha put her finger in the bowl, her finger sat on top of the substance. She said it feels hard and she couldn't get her finger in it. Then I put my fist on it. It was hard. I couldn't get my fist through it. We then wrote down what happened each time and did the same steps two more times. The second trial, Samantha added green coloring and the third trial Miles added blue.

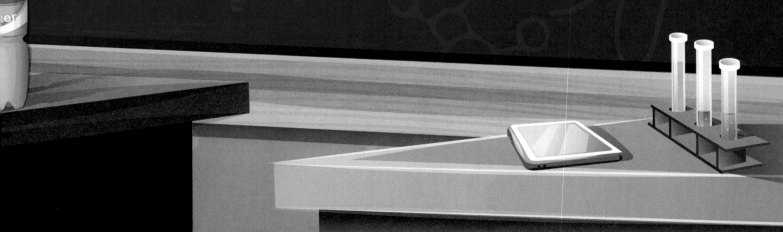

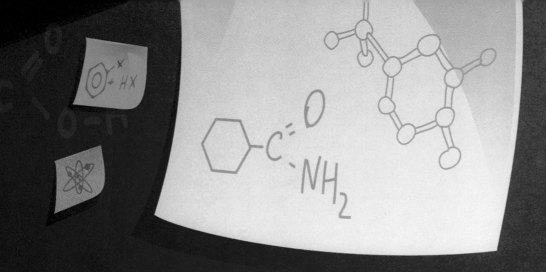

Each time we did the experiment, we got the same results. The bowl of red was exactly the same as the green and blue substances. During Trial 2, I put my whole hand in the substance. It felt wet and it surrounded my open hand. Miles finger would not go into the substance. Samantha's fist did not go through the substance either. During trial 3, Samantha's hand got wet and covered with the substance. Elaine's finger did not go the substance. It was hard to the touch of her finger. And lastly, Miles fist did not go through it. He kept banging his fist on the substance and it was harder than a wall.

We called Mrs. Ferguson over to see what we did. She then told us we had to do step 5. Now that we are on step 5 and we are almost done. We had to analyze or take a look at the data to see what happened and decide if our hypothesis is correct.

Solid

Liquid

Gas

FINAL RESULTS: From reviewing our data, we were a little surprised. We found that our hypothesis was right and wrong. The substance could be a liquid and it could be a solid. At times, it may seem like a solid or a liquid but it acts differently than a normal solid or liquid. When we put our hand in slowly it went right in. When we touched it with our finger or hit it with our fist it was hard.

	Put Your Hand In It What did you feel?	Put Your Finger In It What did you feel?	Put Your Fist In It What did you feel?
RED MIX	Miles – It was a liquid. My open hand went into it and it dripped off my fingers.	Samantha – It was hard and my finger didn't go in it.	Elaine – My fist would not go through it. It felt hard like a rock.
GREEN MIX	Elaine – It was a liquid. It was dripping off my hand.	Miles – Finger sat on top and didn't go in it.	Samantha – My fist did not go through the substance. It sat on top and the substance was hard.
BLUE MIX	Samantha – It was a liquid. My open hand got wet and covered with it.	Elaine – Finger did not go into it. It was hard under my finger.	Miles – My fist did not go through it. I kept banging y fist on the substance and it was harder than a wall.

Now we are at step 6, we report the results and share all that we've learned. You write everything down so someone can follow your steps when it is their turn. We completed a chart to help us analyze the data.

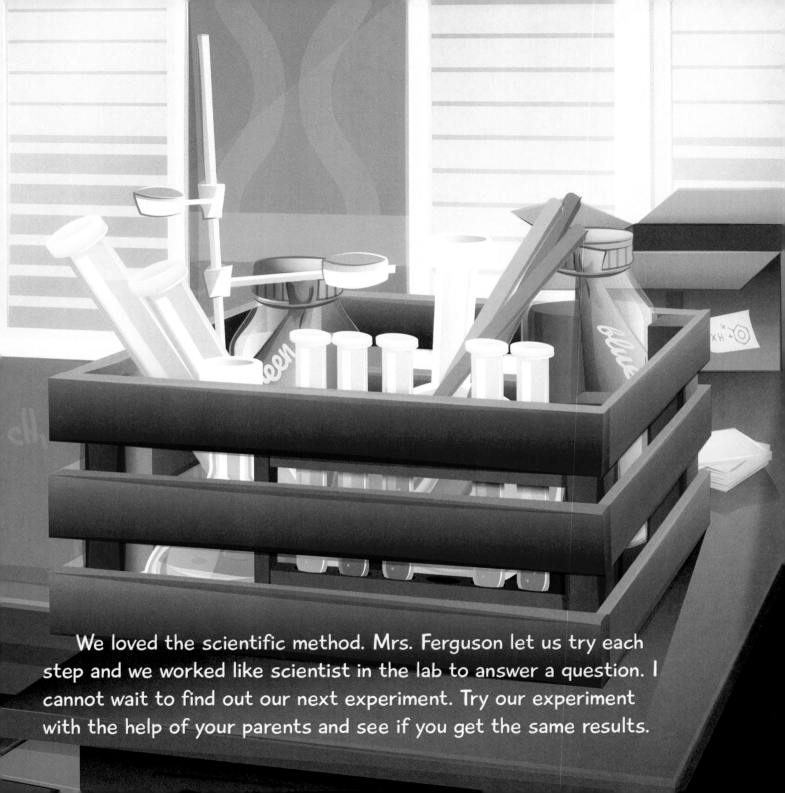

We loved the scientific method. Mrs. Ferguson let us try each step and we worked like scientist in the lab to answer a question. I cannot wait to find out our next experiment. Try our experiment with the help of your parents and see if you get the same results.

Step 2. Do background research:

We did research on matter by reading books and using the internet. We found books on the states of matter. I learned that matter is everything that has weight and takes up space. Matter includes solids, liquids and gases and all of these items can be found in any place. Solids are made of a lot of little particles called molecules. In a solid object the molecules are packed very closely together. Solids have three main properties. A solid has definite volume, definite weight and definite shape that do not easily change.

Samantha focused on the liquid. She told us that liquids have three main properties. A liquid does not have a definite shape, a liquid has a definite mass and a liquid has a definite volume. We learned that a liquid will always take up the same amount of space and take the shape of its container. An example is that water takes the shape of the cup you put it in.

Miles did research on gas. A gas has these three main properties. A gas does not have a definite shape, a gas does not have a definite mass and a gas does not have a definite volume. A gas does not always weigh the same or take up the same amount of space. However, like a liquid, a gas will always take the shape of its container, no matter the size or shape of that container. An example of this is helium in a balloon.

#2

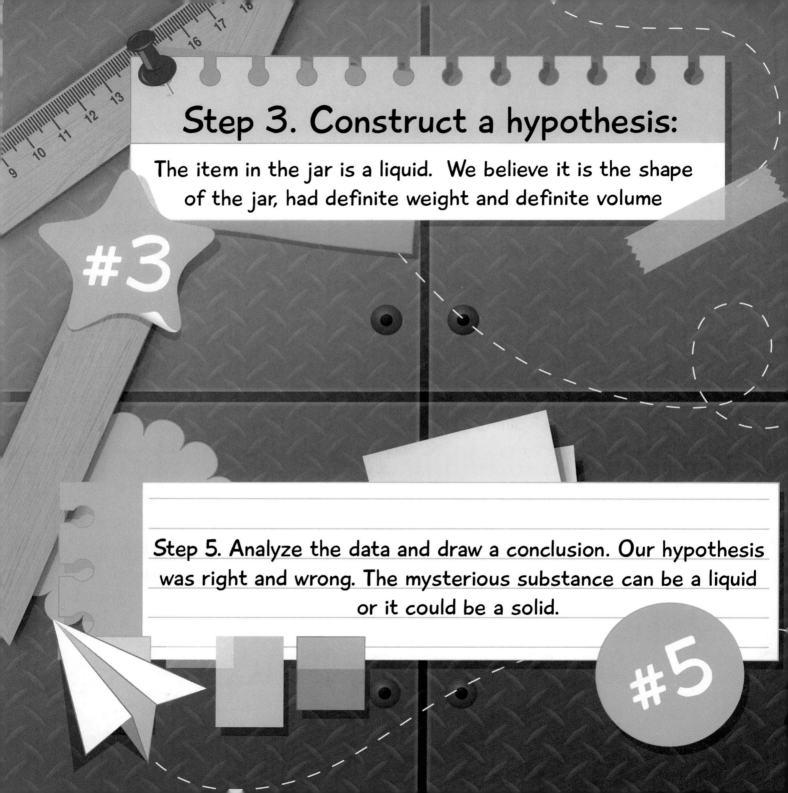

Step 3. Construct a hypothesis:

The item in the jar is a liquid. We believe it is the shape of the jar, had definite weight and definite volume

#3

Step 5. Analyze the data and draw a conclusion. Our hypothesis was right and wrong. The mysterious substance can be a liquid or it could be a solid.

#5

Step 4. Test your hypothesis by doing an experiment

What is It Experiment
Materials: old newspaper, three bowls, three big spoons, a measuring cup, wet wipes, napkins, food coloring with red, green and blue, a box corn starch and two bottles of water.

Procedure

Line the table with newspaper

Put 2 cups of corn starch in a bowl

Add 1 cup of water in the bowl

Add a few drops of red color

Stir up our ingredients

Place your hand into the substance palm flat

Place your finger tip into the substance

Place your fist on the substance.

Do trial 2 using green and trial 3 using blue.

Follow each step of the procedure.

#4

	Put Your Hand In It What did you feel?	Put Your Finger In It What did you feel?	Put Your Fist In It What did you feel?
RED MIX			
GREEN MIX			
BLUE MIX			

FINAL RESULTS:

VISIT
WWW.MCBRIDESTORIES.COM
FOR MORE TITLES

Tia Elaine Keels-Gaymon

Tia Elaine Keels-Gaymon is an educator and entrepreneur, owning several businesses. Mrs. Keels-Gaymon holds a Bachelor's degree in Biology and a Master's Degree in Education with an emphasis in Continuing Education/ Curriculum and Instruction with a Certification in Administration at Coppin State University. She currently is a Professional Development Writer, Trainer, and Facilitator, Mentor, STEM Advocate, STEM Program Developer and STEM Curriculum Writer.

Mrs. Keels-Gaymon started her career as an Educator, later becoming a school administrator and has been in education for over 20 years. After leaving the public school system, Mrs. Keels-Gaymon works as the Curriculum Coordinator for NASA funded Baltimore MUREP Aerospace Academy at Morgan State University.

Throughout her years as an educator, Mrs. Keels- Gaymon has shared her love of STEM education with hundreds of teachers, students and parents. She continues to advocate for STEM education as she works with teachers during school by supporting teachers via Mentoring, Professional Development and Co-teaching in the public and private school sector; provide supports to parents and community members via STEM workshops and activities; and provide out of school hands-on STEM activities for students from Pre-School to Grade 12 with the NASA Baltimore MUREP Aerospace Academy

Mrs. Keels-Gaymon enjoys her work in service of helping others. She is dedicated to increasing participation and retention of historically underrepresented K-12 youth in the fields of science, technology, engineering and mathematics, or STEM; to inspire a more diverse population of students to pursue careers in STEM; engage students, teachers and parents by incorporating emerging technologies; and provide a challenging curriculum that meets state math, science and technology standards. She hopes to encourage children around the world to garner a love for STEM.

Made in the USA
Middletown, DE
13 December 2020